Team Stats—Basketball Edition

CHICAGO BULLS

Nicki Clausen-Grace
and Jeff Grace

BLACK RABBIT BOOKS

Bolt is published by Black Rabbit Books
P.O. Box 227, Mankato, Minnesota, 56002.
www.blackrabbitbooks.com

Jennifer Besel, editor; Michael Sellner, designer;
Omay Ayres, photo researcher

Cataloging-in-Publication Data is available at the Library of Congress
ISBN 978-1-62310-289-0 (hardcover)
ISBN 978-1-64466-385-1 (paperback)
ISBN 978-1-62310-383-5 (e-book)

All facts and statistics are current as of the 2018–2019 season.

Image Credits

Alamy: Danita Delimont, 3; Stephen Chung, 13; AP Images: ASSOCIATED PRESS, 7; Fred Jewell, 28–29; Jeff Robbins, 27; John Swart, 24–25; MICHAEL CONROY, 13; Tom Mihalek, 16–17; bleacherreport.com: Bleacher Report, 10–11; Chicago Bulls Media Guide: Chicago Bulls Public and Media Relations, 8–9; commons.wikimedia.org: Fma12, 7; Dreamstime: Maxim Grebeshkov, 18–19; Facebook: Stadium, 4–5; Getty: Bettmann, 18; Hulton Archive, 21; Paul Natkin, 22–23; Tom Smart, 15; Newscom: Gary A. Vasquez/USA TODAY Sports, Cover; NUCCIO DINUZZO/KRT, 12; Rob Tringali SportsChrome, 14; Shutterstock: Duda Vasilii, 28–29; EFKS, Cover, 1; GOLFX, 31; IfH, Cover; vasosh, 12, 17, 22–23, 28–29, 32; Tumblir: meezumaki, 11
Every effort has been made to contact copyright holders for material reproduced in this book. Any omissions will be rectified in subsequent printings if notice is given to the publisher.

CONTENTS

JORDAN
23
CAVS
43
NBA
HUFFY

On the COURT

It was Game 5 of the 1989 Eastern Conference NBA **playoffs**. There were three seconds left in the game. The Cleveland Cavaliers led the Chicago Bulls 100–99. Then Bulls star Michael Jordan got the ball. He turned and sank it. Bulls won!

History of the BULLS

The Chicago Bulls team has played strong since it began in 1966. It made the playoffs its first season. And it didn't stop there. In the 1995–1996 season, the Bulls won 72 out of 82 games. It was the first team to win more than 70 games in a season.

1966 team

Teams Worth the Most Money

(as of 2018)

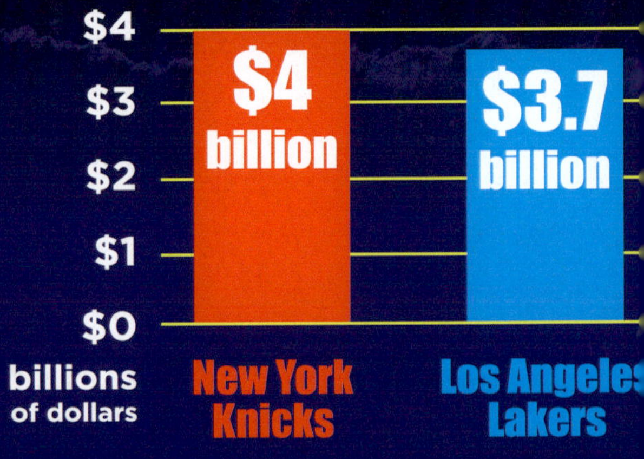

Money Makers

The Bulls team does more than play ball. It also earns a lot of money. In 2018, it was worth $2.9 billion. That was the fourth-highest **net worth** in the NBA. Teams make money through ticket sales and TV deals. They also sell items with the team **logo** on them.

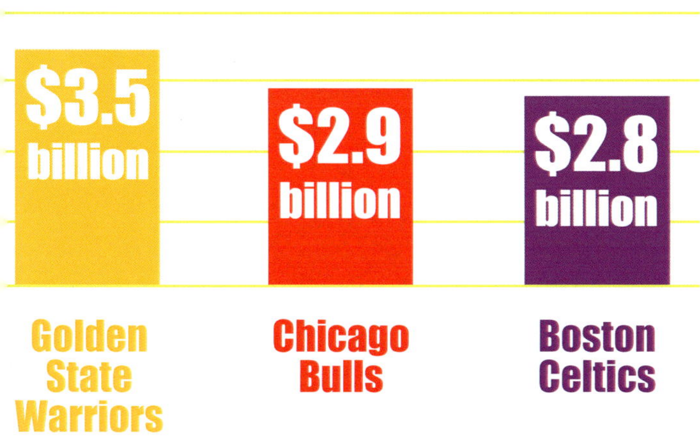

CHAPTER 3

Greatest MOMENTS

Fans love to remember some of the team's great moments. One of those was Game 6 of the 1992 Finals. The team was down 15 points. It had just one quarter left. Bulls player Scottie Pippen came out hot. He started scoring and creating **turnovers**. With about five minutes left, he tied the game. That gave the team the boost it needed. The players fought hard and won a second NBA Championship.

Scottie Pippen

The Bulls' mascot is Benny the Bull. It was the first NBA mascot.

Another Title

In the 1997 Finals, the Bulls led three games to two against the Utah Jazz. Game 6 was tied 86–86. There were less than 10 seconds left. Michael Jordan passed the ball to Steve Kerr. Kerr sank the shot, giving the Bulls the lead. The Bulls won its fifth NBA title.

Three in a Row

In 1998, history repeated itself. It was Game 6 of the Finals. The Bulls played the Jazz again. With 30 seconds left, the Bulls trailed by one point. Michael Jordan stole the ball from Jazz player Karl Malone. Then he hit the game-winning shot. The Bulls won 87–86. It was the team's third championship in a row.

In 1993, Jordan retired from the NBA. He went to play minor-league baseball. But he returned to the Bulls in 1995. And he led the team to three straight NBA championships.

JORDAN
23
JAZZ
32

Bulls Team Records

By the Numbers

130–74
score of biggest **win**

72
most **wins** in a season

77–133
score of biggest **loss**

168
most points
scored in
a game
15 fewest
wins
in a season
49 fewest
points
scored
in a game

Retired Jerseys

No Bulls player will wear these numbers again.

CHAPTER 4

BULLS Superstars

The team charges onto the court with amazing players. Jerry Sloan was one of those players. He played 10 seasons with the team. He **averaged** 14.7 points and 7.7 rebounds per game. Fans loved his **aggressive** style of play.

Michael Jordan

Michael Jordan is one of the all-time greats. Most players are never named the NBA **MVP**. Jordan earned the title five times.

Jordan still holds many team records. He has the most points, **assists**, steals, free throws, and games played.

Bulls Team Leaders for Most Points Scored

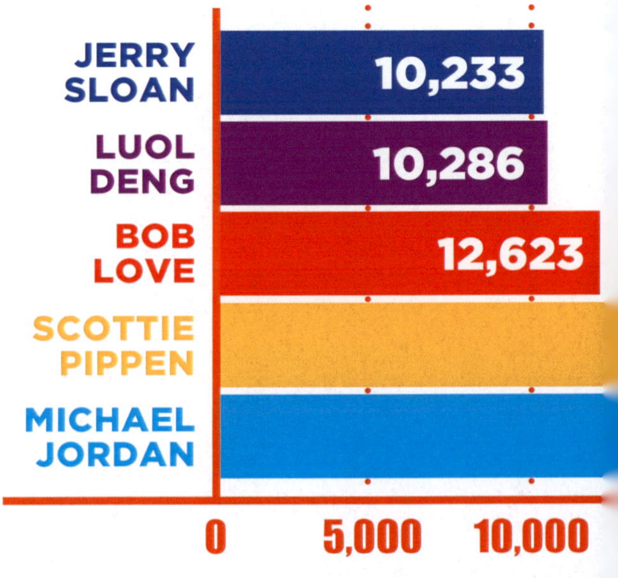

BULLS
15,123
29,277
15,000
20,000
25,000
30,000

BULLS LEADERS IN BASKETS MADE

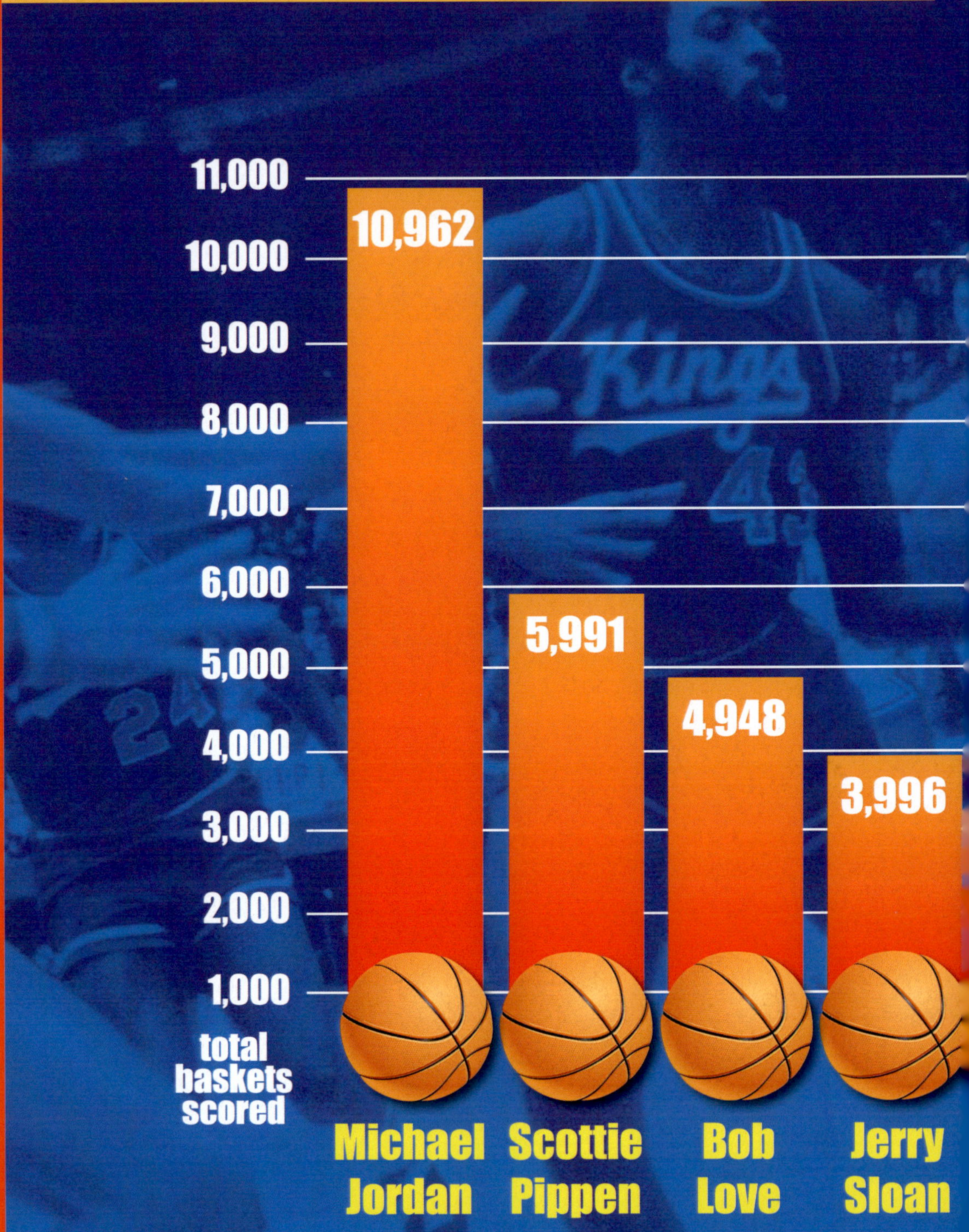

3,987
Luol Deng
3,558
Chet Walker
3,466
Artis Gilmore
3,102
Derrick Rose
3,101
Kirk Hinrich
3,047
Reggie Theus

NEW YORK
14
BULLS

Scottie Pippen

Scottie Pippen was known as Michael Jordan's sidekick. They worked very well together. Pippen ranks second in Bulls history on points scored, assists, and steals. In 1996, Pippen was named one of the NBA's 50 Greatest Players.

Coach Phil Jackson

Players can't win games all by themselves. They need skilled coaches to help them. Phil Jackson was a great coach. He led the Bulls in all six of its NBA championships. In his Bulls career, Jackson won 545 games. That's more than any other Bulls coach.

The Bulls have a strong history. With great players and coaches, the team will continue to charge ahead.

Jackson was named one of the 10 greatest coaches in NBA history.

BULLS TIMELINE

1966

The team forms.

1978

Sloan is the first Bulls player to have his jersey number retired.

1984

Team drafts Jordan.

1989

Jackson becomes head coach.

1991

Bulls win its first NBA championship.

1998

Bulls win its sixth NBA championship.

2018

The team is valued at \$2.9 billion. It's the fourth-highest value in the NBA.

GLOSSARY

aggressive (uh-GRES-iv)—showing a readiness to fight, argue, or attack

assist (uh-SIST)—the action, such as a pass, of a player who helps a teammate to score

average (AHV-rij)—a number that is calculated by adding quantities together and then dividing the total by the number of quantities

logo (LO-go)—a symbol used to identify a company

mascot (MAH-scaht)—a person, animal, or object adopted by a group as a symbolic figure especially to bring them good luck

MVP—an award given to the best player in the league each season; MVP stands for most valuable player.

net worth (NEHT WURTH)—the amount of money someone would have after selling everything and paying all their bills

playoff (PLAY-ahf)—a series of games played after the regular season to decide which player or team is the champion

turnover (TURN-oh-vur)—the act of a team losing possession of a ball

BOOKS

Anderson, Kirsten. *Who Is Michael Jordan?* Who Was? New York: Penguin Workshop, 2019.

Flynn, Brendan. *Chicago Bulls All-Time Greats.* Mankato, MN: Press Room Editions, 2020.

Goodman, Michael E. *Chicago Bulls.* NBA Champions. Mankato, MN: Creative Education, 2018.

WEBSITES

Chicago Bulls
www.britannica.com/topic/Chicago-Bulls

Chicago Bulls
www.nba.com/bulls/

Chicago Bulls History
history.bulls.com/#firstPage

INDEX